DRAGON'S Merry Christmas

DAV PILKEY

ORCHARD BOOKS

An Imprint of Scholastic Inc./New York

THE DRAGON TALES

Copyright © 1991 by Dav Pilkey
All rights reserved. Published by Orchard Books,
an imprint of Scholastic Inc. ORCHARD BOOKS and design
are registered trademarks of Watts Publishing Group, Ltd.,
used under license. SCHOLASTIC and associated logos are
trademarks and/or registered trademarks of Scholastic Inc..

Library of Congress Cataloging-in-Publication Data
Pilkey, Dav, / date.   Dragon's Merry Christmas.
Dragon's third tale / Dav Pilkey   p. cm.   (The Dragon tales)
Summary: Dragon has a merry time in the Christmas season,
decorating a tree outdoors, making a chocolate candy wreath,
and sharing his Christmas gifts with needy animals.
ISBN-10: 0-439-54848-9 / ISBN-13: 978-0-439-54848-9 (pbk.)
[I. Dragons—Fiction. 2. Christmas—Fiction.]
I. Title   II. Series Dragon Tales.
PZ7.P63123Dt 1991 [E]—dc20   91001996
20 19 18 17 16 15 14 13   15 16 17 18/0
Printed in the U.S.A.   40
The illustrations are watercolor with pencil,
reproduced in full color.
This Orchard Books edition, October 2007

Contents

For Linda and
Amelie Anderson

1
The Perfect Christmas Tree

One cold morning, Dragon went out
to find the perfect Christmas tree.
He walked through the crunchy snow.

He saw all sorts of trees . . .
big ones, small ones,
crooked ones, and straight ones.

Finally, he found the most beautiful
Christmas tree of all.
It was not too big,
or too small. . . .
It was not too crooked,
or too straight.
It was just right.

Dragon looked down and saw
the tree's beautiful brown trunk.
It stood firm and strong
in the frozen earth.

He looked up and saw
its beautiful green branches.
They waved back and forth
in the cold December wind.

Dragon could not cut down
such a lovely tree.

11

Instead, he came back
with colored lights, silver bells . . .

. . . and everything he needed
to make his tree even more beautiful.

That night, Dragon looked out
at his Christmas tree
shining in the night.
It was truly perfect.

2
The Candy Wreath

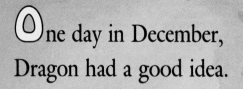

One day in December,
Dragon had a good idea.

"I will make a wreath out of candy,"
he said.

Dragon took some old wire
and bent it into shape.
Then he taped little pieces
of chocolate candy all around it.

When Dragon hung his candy wreath
on the wall, one of the pieces
of chocolate fell off.
Dragon picked it up and ate it.
It was very good.

Dragon did not want his wreath
to look bare, so he promised
not to eat any more candy.
"I will eat only the pieces
that fall off," he said.

Dragon bumped his elbow against the wall,
and two more pieces of candy
fell off.

"Whoops," he said, gobbling them up.

Dragon sat down in his chair
and looked up at his candy wreath.
He tried not to think about
the smooth,
rich,
sweet,
creamy,
dark chocolate candy.

Dragon could not sit still.
He began to drool.

Suddenly, Dragon could not stop himself.
He shook the candy wreath
back and forth . . .

. . . and then jumped up and down on it,
until every last piece of candy
had fallen off.

Dragon got a tummy ache
from eating so much chocolate.

"Next year," said Dragon,
"I will make my wreath
out of pinecones."

3

Mittens

Dragon was always losing
his mittens.
No matter how hard he tried,
he could never keep track of them.
Whenever he needed them most,
they were nowhere to be found.

So Dragon went out and bought
a pair of clip-on mittens.

He clipped them to his coat sleeves,
so he would never lose his mittens
again.

Then he lost his coat.

4
Merry Christmas, Dragon

Dragon loved Christmas.
Every year he saved his money,
and every Christmas
he bought wonderful presents
for himself.

Dragon made a list of the things
he would buy.

1. Lots of food.
2. a new coat.
3. a big birdhouse.

Then Dragon wrapped himself up
in a warm quilt
and headed off to the store.

When Dragon finished his Christmas
shopping, the store clerk
loaded everything into a big sack.

On his way home, Dragon passed
some raccoons singing in the street.

The raccoons had no food to eat.
They looked very hungry.

Dragon reached into his sack
and took out his big basket of food.
"Merry Christmas," said Dragon.

Then he passed an old rhino
shoveling her sidewalk.
The rhino did not have a coat to wear.
She looked very cold.

Dragon reached into his sack
and took out his new wool overcoat.

"Merry Christmas," said Dragon.

Finally, Dragon saw two little birds
sitting on a branch.
The birds did not have a home to live in.
They looked very sad.

Dragon opened his big sack,
took out his birdhouse,
and hung it on a branch.

"Merry Christmas," said Dragon.

When Dragon got home,
his big sack was empty.

There were no presents left for him.
But Dragon did not feel sad.

He went upstairs to his quiet room
and crawled beneath his soft warm quilt.

And later, as he slept,
Dragon dreamed he heard angels
singing in the starry night.